This book belongs to:

Weather or Not

Disney's Out & About With Pooh
A Grow and Learn Library

Published by Advance Publishers
© 1996 Disney Enterprises, Inc.
Based on the Pooh stories by A. A. Milne © The Pooh Properties Trust.
All rights reserved. Printed in the United States.
No part of this book may be reproduced or copied in any form
without written permission from the copyright owner.

Written by Ann Braybrooks
Illustrated by Arkadia Illustration Ltd.
Designed by Vickey Bolling
Produced by Bumpy Slide Books

ISBN:1-885222-64-5
10 9 8 7 6

On a sunny morning in spring, Pooh listened to Owl talk about the weather.

Owl said, "No wind or precipitation today!"

"Pre-what?" asked Pooh.

"Precipitation," said Owl. "Rain, Pooh. It definitely will not rain today."

Pooh was very glad. He was so glad that he had an idea. "Would you like to go on a picnic?" he asked Owl.

"I'm sorry, Pooh," said Owl, "but I promised to have tea with my aunt."

As Owl flew off, Pooh headed down the path toward
Piglet's. He found his friend in the front yard, fluffing a rug.
"Hello, Piglet," said Pooh. "How about a picnic?"
"No, thank you," said Piglet. "I have spring cleaning to do."

"Oh," said Pooh, as a droopy look came over his face. Then he brightened. "You could do your spring cleaning tomorrow," he suggested. "I'll even help you."

Piglet looked at the rug, then at Pooh. "All right, Pooh," said Piglet. "Let me get my picnic things."

"Hooray!" said Pooh. "I'll pack my things, too. Let's meet here in half an hour, or thereabouts, whichever comes first."

Pooh ran down the path as fast as he could. He rushed so fast that he didn't watch where he was going.

"Oof!" said Eeyore as Pooh bumped straight into him. "Hello to you, too!"

"I'm sorry, Eeyore," said Pooh. "I didn't see you."
"I know," Eeyore said gloomily. "No one ever does."
"But now that I *do* see you," said Pooh, "I'd like to invite you to a picnic."

"Me?" asked Eeyore.

"Yes, you!" said Pooh.

"Why, thank you," said Eeyore. "I accept."

"Good!" said Pooh. "Wait here while I get some things. I'll be right back."

At home, Pooh stuffed a basket with a blanket, a few napkins, and three pots of honey.

"I know Piglet will bring haycorn muffins for himself," he said, "and Eeyore will find some thistles to eat. But I'll bring three pots of honey — one for each of us — just in case." Then, at the last minute, Pooh added some bread and jam and tied up the bulging basket with string.

He hurried back to Eeyore, and the two friends trotted down the path to Piglet's. When they arrived, Piglet was outside waiting for them.

As the three friends chatted and strolled through the forest, the conversation rolled around to the weather. Eeyore couldn't help asking, "Are you sure it won't rain?"

"No presipping today," said Pooh, rather boldly.

"No what?" said Eeyore.

"No rain," said Pooh. "Owl said so."

"But what about those?" Piglet squeaked. He pointed to some thin gray smudges in the distant sky.

Pooh squinted. "That may be smoke," he said. "Or dust. But not clouds. Especially not rain clouds."

"Harrumph!" snorted Eeyore doubtfully.

Soon the friends arrived at a lovely, sun-warmed meadow. "Look, Eeyore," said Pooh. "There's some thistle for you, right over there."

As Eeyore went over to taste the thistle, Pooh and
Piglet spread out the picnic blanket nearby.

"It's a beautiful day for a picnic," said Piglet.

"Indeed," said Pooh. "Would you like some honey?"

"No, thank you," said Piglet. "I'll have some bread and jam to start."

"Indeed," said Pooh. "Indeed" was a word that Pooh had just learned from Owl, and Pooh was practicing using it.

Pooh and Piglet began to eat. After every few bites, they politely dabbed the honey and jam off their faces with their napkins.

As Piglet dabbed at his face for the third time, the napkin flew out of his grasp and tumbled toward the trees. As he scurried after it, Piglet cried, "What did Owl say about wind?"

Pooh called, "He said there wasn't going to be any!"

As Piglet returned with the napkin, he asked, "Then what was that?"

Pooh thought. "A flap of air?" he suggested.

"It's wind," insisted Eeyore, looking up from his thistle.

"Only wind makes things flap."

Eeyore was right. By now Pooh could see that Eeyore's ears, along with his mane, were flapping in the wind. And when Pooh stood up, the picnic blanket flapped around his feet, too.

Pooh grabbed a honey pot and said, "Here, Piglet. Help me put a honey pot on each corner of the blanket."

"But we have four corners," said Piglet, "and only three pots!"

"Oh, bother!" cried Pooh. "We'll have to stand on the empty corner."

As Pooh and Piglet secured the blanket, first with the
honey pots, then with themselves, the wind blew around
them. Along with Eeyore, the two friends squeezed their
eyes shut, waiting for the gale to die down.

Finally they were able to open their eyes. Pooh looked at the grass swaying gently in the breeze and said, "It's more breezy than windy now. Why don't we fly kites?"

"What kites?" Piglet asked.

"The ones we can make with our napkins," Pooh said. "I got the idea when I saw your napkin blow away."

Piglet glanced up at the sky, which seemed to be getting darker. "Oh, dear. Are you sure we'll be able to fly kites?" he said. "It's starting to look like rain."

"It sure is," Eeyore offered, although no one had asked him.

Pooh said, "The sky may look like rain is coming, but rain isn't rain until it falls in drops. Until it does, we might as well have fun." Then he smiled. "Anyway, Owl did say that it wouldn't rain today."

So as Piglet and Eeyore watched, Pooh set about making the kites. He used sticks for the frames and the twine from his basket for the lines.

"My kite's kind of nice," Piglet said. "Even with the jam stains."

"What about mine?" complained Eeyore. "It looks awfully plain."

"Hmm," said Pooh. "Let me rub it on the grass to make it green."

Once Eeyore's kite was properly decorated, Pooh helped his friends launch their kites. Then he launched his own. Under the dusky gray sky, they watched their kites bob and weave in the wind.

Suddenly Pooh felt his nose twitch. Or rather, he
felt it itch. Or possibly something had tickled it. Then he felt
himself being tickled all over. There was no mistaking it.
"Oh, bother!" Pooh cried. "Rain!"

As the drops fell, the friends pulled their kites out of the sky. "The picnic's over," said Eeyore. "I'm not surprised."

"Don't be so gloomy, Eeyore!" urged Pooh. "Let's wait awhile and see if it clears up."

Pooh walked over to the picnic blanket and said, "In the meantime, Piglet, help me make a tent. I'll drape the blanket over a branch, then we'll stand underneath and hold up the sides. Eeyore can stand in the middle so he doesn't get wet."

A short while later, the wind and the rain stopped, and the sun came out again.

"I think I'll go home," said Eeyore, stepping out from under the tent. "All this weather has made me sleepy."

Pooh wanted him to stay, but remembered that when Eeyore didn't get his rest, he was even less cheerful than usual.

"Thank you for coming to our picnic!" Pooh called after his friend.

After Eeyore was gone, Piglet said, "What should we do now? I have some of my muffin left."

"I have half a pot of honey left," said Pooh. "Shall we finish them?"

"Why not?" said Piglet.

"Why not?" echoed Pooh. He looked at the blanket hanging over the branch. "We can take down the tent and sit on the dry grass underneath."

"Good idea," said Piglet.

"Indeed!" said Pooh.

So Pooh and Piglet sat, finishing their picnic.
As they ate, they gazed at the raindrops glistening
on the leaves of the trees.

"You know, Pooh," said Piglet, "any day is a good
day for a picnic — as long as you share it with friends."

"It certainly is," said Pooh. "Weather or not!"